LYNX TWINS GROW UP

by Stephanie Smith

Illustrated by Robert Hynes

Little® Soundprints

To Dr. Staples and Dr. Calabrese, who taught me to read, write, and speak—S.S.

To my family—R.H.

Published by Soundprints, an imprint of Trudy Corporation, Norwalk, Connecticut.

Book design: Marcin D. Pilchowski
Editor: Laura Gates Galvin
Editorial assistance: Chelsea Shriver

First Edition 2002
10 9 8 7 6 5 4
Printed in China

Acknowledgments:
　　　　Our very special thanks to Dr. Don E. Wilson of the Department of Systematic Biology at the Smithsonian Institution's National Museum of Natural History for his curatorial review, and our very special thanks to Robert Hynes for his amazing work under pressure.
　　　　Soundprints would also like to thank Ellen Nanney and Robyn Bissette at the Smithsonian Institution's Office of Product Development and Licensing for their help in the creation of this book.
　　　　The author wishes to thank Linda Ferraresso for her expertise on birds.

Library of Congress Cataloging-in-Publication Data

Smith, Stephanie, 1976-
Lynx twins grow up / by Stephanie Smith ; illustrated by Robert Hynes.
　　　　　　　p. cm.
Summary: Two lynx kittens learn to care for themselves and avoid danger in their forest home.
ISBN 1-931465-20-7 (hardcover) — ISBN 1-931465-19-3 (pbk.)
1. Lynx—Juvenile fiction. [1. Lynx—Fiction. 2. Animals—Infancy—Fiction.] I. Hynes, Robert, ill. II. Title.

PZ10.3.S6548 Ly 2002
[Fic]—dc21

2001049688

Table of Contents

A note to the reader:

Throughout this story you will see words in **bold letters**. There is more information about these words in the glossary. The glossary is in the back of the book.

Chapter 1
Lynx Kittens Are Born

It is a sunny spring day in the forest. Two lynx kittens are born in a hollow log. One kitten is a boy. The other kitten is a girl. Their nest is cozy and safe.

The lynx twins and their mother live in the **boreal forest**. Moose, bears and other creatures live there, too. The twins can hear **chickadees** singing in the tall spruce trees.

The twins sleep most of the day. Their thick gray fur keeps them warm, even on cold nights. Mother Lynx stays by their side to protect them from danger.

One night, the lynx twins wake up from their nap. Mother Lynx is gone. But they are not afraid. They know she is hunting food. The twins wait in the **den** for Mother Lynx to return. She brings them a squirrel to eat.

In May, the lynx twins are ready to leave the den. They follow Mother Lynx through the forest. They **stalk** insects. They wrestle, roll and tumble with each other. They are playing. They are also learning to be hunters.

Chapter 2

Learning to Hunt

The lynx twins and Mother Lynx are out in the forest. Mother Lynx is hunting. She stalks a snowshoe hare. She knows the hare is hiding under a bush. She is about to **pounce**.

The twins play near their mother. The male kitten sees a **spruce grouse** on the ground. He crouches low, just like his mother. Then he pounces. But he is not fast enough! Brother Lynx chases the bird up a tree. He has never climbed a tree before!

Brother Lynx cannot catch the bird. He jumps to the ground and pounces on his sister. The twins tumble and play. They are very noisy! The hare hears them and runs away.

Mother Lynx chases the hare. But she cannot catch it this time. The lynx twins follow Mother Lynx to another part of the woods. Mother Lynx will begin her hunt again.

Chapter 3

Forest Adventure

In September, the lynx twins learn to hunt. They watch Mother Lynx and do what she does. Sometimes they catch mice or bugs. Soon their teeth will grow strong. Soon they will hunt bigger animals.

The lynx family hunts after dark. One night, Mother Lynx stops suddenly. She knows that danger is near. She smells the air. She hears a sound. The twins are still and quiet, like Mother Lynx.

They can all hear the sound now. Something big is running toward them! Brother Lynx runs up a tree. His sister stays very still.

A moose crashes through the trees. A gray wolf is chasing him. The wolf sees Sister Lynx. He knows she is easier to catch than the moose. He lets the moose run away.

Mother Lynx runs at the wolf. The wolf turns away from Sister Lynx. He chases Mother Lynx. She is fast and runs up a large tree. Sister Lynx climbs up another tree. Everyone is safe!

The wolf paces. He barks and growls at the lynx family. They stay still and quiet in the trees. The wolf knows that he will not catch them now. He trots away. The danger has finally passed.

Chapter 4

All Grown Up

November arrives. The air is crisp and cool. The lynx twins have grown bigger. Their thick fur will keep them warm all winter. Their teeth and claws are now sharp. They can hunt as well as Mother Lynx.

Sometimes the lynx twins see a male lynx near their mother. She usually chases him away. Today she does not. This older male is her mate. Soon it will be time for Mother Lynx to have babies again.

It is time for the twins to live on their own. Mother Lynx has taught them well. They can take care of themselves. Brother and Sister Lynx run into the forest together.

The twins stay together. They protect each other. They share food and a den. In spring, the twins will separate and live on their own. They will start their own families. They will take care of their kittens and teach them to live in the boreal forest.

Glossary

Boreal forest: a region of thick fir and spruce trees. A boreal forest is found in the northern parts of Canada and Alaska.

Chickadee: a type of bird found in the boreal forest.

Den: a place where certain animals find safety and store food.

Pounce: to suddenly approach and capture an animal.

Spruce grouse: a bird that lives mostly in thick spruce forests.

Stalk: to hunt slowly and quietly.

Wilderness Facts
About the Lynx

The Canadian lynx is from the cat family. Lynx have long legs, a short tail, and tufts of fur at the tips of their ears. Lynx kittens look just like house cats when they are first born.

The male lynx does not live with the family. Lynx kittens depend on their mother for everything. Their mother catches food and protects them. When lynx are about six months old, the baby teeth they were born with, called milk teeth, are replaced with stronger teeth. Soon after their stronger teeth come in, they are full-grown. They can hunt and take care of themselves.

Lynx stay in their den most of the day and go outside at night. The darkness hides them from predators who are looking for food of their own to eat. Lynx eat snowshoe hares, grouse, squirrels and other rodents. Lynx live in the northern boreal forest. The boreal forest is a large region that covers much of Canada and Alaska. It is made up of thick fir and spruce trees.

Other animals that are found in the boreal forest include:

Beavers

Black bears

Chickadees

Ermines

Gray wolves

Great horned owls

Moose

Red foxes

Snowshoe hares

Snowy owls

Spruce grouse

Squirrels